Capturing moments through Photography

Juan Moisés de la Serna

Translator: Emma Rowe

Editorial Tektime

2022

"Capturando el momento con una Fotografía"

Written by Juan Moisés de la Serna

Translator: Emma Rowe

1st edition: August 2022

Prologue

It was an icy morning: one of those where you want to stay in bed until the sunlight forces you to get up.

I looked around me, contemplating the framed photographs on my bedroom walls. There were maybe a hundred, or maybe more: I had lost count. They were all framed: white, black blue... made out of wood, brass, silver... in an effort to make each one unique, different from the rest.

Dedicated to my parents

Index

CHAPTER 1. MY FIRST JOB

Life goes fast, even if you don't want it to

Just look behind you and you will see the past.

It follows you wherever you go,

Closer everyday, taking years from your life.

Never ending, taking away things you love:

caresses and kisses, that day you shared

The past took it away, I don't know where to find it,

Just in his image left in a portrait.

His affectionate words silenced,

His morning kisses and his caresses at dusk, gone.

Silenced without warning.

My entire life changed in an instant.

So many unsaid words, kissed undelivered,

Caresses still needed and everything remaining in the
past.

A promise made to live together eternally,

Unaccomplished: the past arrived.

Nobody seems to care what the past stole,

It's going to separate me from my life, leaving me without
him.

The photos will remain where memory begins to falter,

It's the past's fault.

LOVE

It was an icy morning, one of those where you want to stay in bed until the sunlight forces you to get up.

I looked around me, contemplating the framed photographs on my bedroom walls. There were maybe a hundred, or maybe more: I had lost count. They were all framed: white, black blue... made out of wood, brass, silver... in an effort to make each one unique, different from the rest. Each one of those photos was a memory, or at least had tried to be, a moment, an image of the present turned into the past in an instant. I don't know what to call it, maybe an obsession, but I had a need for it: to immortalise people, to keep their memory alive so that in time someone could see them and know what they had done. But it was only an illusion.

It all started in a small photography company, one of those ones next to a police station for people who were going to renew their ID card or passport; the ones that were swapped for automatic machines which gave you a lower quality photo for a lower price but served the same purpose. I didn't know anything about that business, but I didn't want to be any more of a burden on my parents than I already was. They put in a lot of effort to pay for me to go to university and they insisted that I concentrate on my studies and enjoy my time as a student. They had always told me that the important thing in life was what you achieved, the position you got and how much money you earnt so that's why I tried to make a good impression on the boss in this job: my first job. I arrived an hour early and was the last to leave. Although the salary was not high and they didn't pay me for those extra hours, at least it allowed me to help my family, even a little, in lightening the cost of my studies. So without meaning to, I was introduced to the world of photography, or rather: portraiture. It wasn't complicated. Before taking the picture you only had to sit someone on a pre-prepared, well lit chair and then ask them to smile. Then afterwards collect their information and tell them to come back in an hour to allow the photo to develop. An activity I dedicated a few hours a day to, my main occupation being that of a student: attending classes, note taking, doing homework, handing in exercises and studying.

At first I didn't even pay attention to what I was doing. "Please sit here", "please smile", "wait a moment" and "ready". But everything changed when a serious and timid lady came in.

"Goodday, madam, can I help?" I said with a big smile.

"I've come for a photo."

"Yes, of course, please tell me the receipt number."

"What receipt number?" asked the woman, surprised.

"When an order is placed a receipt is given with a number on it. That's what I am asking for."

"I don't know anything about a number and I have placed no order." She replied, annoyed.

"Then are you here to either have some photos taken or have a reel developed?"

"No, no, what I want is to collect some photos." The

petit woman became somewhat agitated.

"Okay, then if you give me the name the photos are under I can look for the number." I said, puzzled.

"I know that but it's not for me."

"They aren't your photos?" I asked, surprised.

"No, well.. Yes…"

"Madam, if it's someone else's photo it needs to be that person who picks it up."

"That's what I'm talking about." She stated as she put her bag on the counter and started to look for something inside.

"Explain, please, because I don't understand."

"Well you see, my husband passed away." She said, shutting her bag.

"My condolences."

"Thank you, but it has been almost a year."

"Okay, so what does that have to do with the photos?"

"Well, I'll tell you. In the weeks after his death I was so angry because he had cheated on me that I tore up his pictures." She said in a rather angry tone.

"He cheated on you?"

"Yes, I can't call it anything else. He promised me eternal love, that we would be together for the rest of our lives, that we would grow old together and look at me now. He abandoned me, left me alone, I won't have anyone to share old age with."

"Well Madam, I'm not sure I consider that cheating."

"Why not? He swore it before a judge and God."

"But I don't think your husband decided to cheat you…"

"No, I understand that, it was Cancer that took him."

"Okay, so…?"

"Even so he should have stayed with me, not left me all alone."

"I understand your point but I still don't understand why you're here…?"

"Oh! Yes, well as I was saying, at first I felt very bad for that betrayal and I tore his things and his photos because I hurt every time I saw them."

"Yes, you said."

"Well what I'm saying is that over time I tried not to think about him, tried not to remember him so that I would hurt less."

"And did it work?" I asked, curious.

"What do you think? Of course not! It's like saying you're not going to think about your right hand, even though it's still attached to you, even though it's still there."

"What happened?"

"Well over time I tried to do the opposite of that, I tried to recover as many memories as possible."

"Memories, what sort of memories?"

"Well I went to the places I had been with him, and tried to eat the same things, and buy the same souvenirs from those places."

"And did that work?"

"No, on the contrary I felt a knot in my stomach when I arrived in the city on the bus and remembered every corner that I passed by with him." She said sadly.

"And what about the food?"

"I tried, I tried many times, but it was impossible for me to eat the same things we ate and I spent hours staring at the plate without trying the food. I don't know why, but I didn't want to be there without my husband, and it only made the pain worse: realising that I was alone and that he was never coming back."

"But I still don't understand... What does that have to do with the photos?"

"As I said I destroyed them all thinking that... I don't know... that it would make me feel better, make me forget... or... I don't know what I was thinking. In any case, it left me with no photos of my husband and I am trying to recover them."

"Recover them? How? Do you have a camera with the negatives on?"

"No, I tore them all up." she said in a sad low voice.

"Then how will you recover them?"

"Well I am visiting all the photography houses that I remember that we went to, to see if they kept an image of my husband."

"But Madam, how can that be possible?"

"Because it can't not be!" she exclaimed, upset.

"But we photograph thousands of clients a year and we don't save them all."

"But you haven't even looked."

"I can try and have a look but I'm telling you I don't think it's possible."

"Yes please, have a look. I hope I'm lucky because this is my ninth photography house and none of the others gave me a positive answer."

"Because what you're asking for is impossible." I replied.

"Impossible or not, I have an important need to be close to my husband and the only way I think I can do it is through the photos."

"Well, I can ask my boss."

"Yes please, I would be very grateful. The truth is that I haven't been lucky up to now, I haven't found even one little photo and it's very important to me."

After giving me all the details she could about the approximate date that her husband could have had the photo taken, she left.

That encounter made me reflect on the importance of the job I was doing and even though the majority of the time my activity was limited to taking photos and spending hours developing them, the thought that I could help that woman made me feel good. The truth is, I don't know how I would react in that situation, if my soul mate suddenly died overnight. Although in this case she had at least had some time to say goodbye, if you can call it that since it seems the Cancer advanced rapidly. He, however, didn't have time to say goodbye. His last words were "I love you" and then that was it. At least that's how the woman confessed it to me, crying all the while. All that sounded foreign to me since I hadn't gone through the death of a loved one. I understood the suffering she was going through and her determination to recover the memory of her love, although I wasn't sure if finding those images would ease her pain. She was wrong when she destroyed her husband's photos because she felt a deep sense of betrayal and abandonment at the sight of them. I don't know if recovering the images now will give her what she wants.

After telling the story to my boss, he told me not to bother looking for the pictures because the woman would probably not come back. But my boss was wrong, not only did the woman return that day, but the following day and the day after that, until I asked her not to return. I don't know why but the woman had the impression that I didn't want to help her and that I didn't try hard enough to find her husband's picture. What the woman had to bear in mind was that a year ago I was not in that job, so I did not know who her husband was or where the photos could be. According to my boss, after talking to him more than once, there was no way to locate the photos since they were not kept in the archives for long. I tried looking anyway: by first name, surname and even by some characteristics the woman had told me, but it was impossible.

That a photo could mean so much was surprising for someone who could take ten or twenty photos on a good day. The people didn't pay much attention either because they only used them to carry out paperwork for official sites. Although it's true that the photography office also offered other services like wedding or communion photos or for other social events. That was not part of my job, it was the job of external staff related to the boss. I didn't really know what kind of relationship they had but I suppose he would take a percentage cut. Of course, apart from the photos that were taken there was also the development service, a service that had changed a lot in recent years according to the boss. So although previously it was quite artisanal, nowadays everything was done automatically by machine, you just had to make sure you put the first image on the reel in the right place. This was a simple job for a very basic salary but it allowed me to pay expenses, and despite the fact that my introduction to the world of photography was for economic reasons, over the years it led to a whole life experience that I will relate in this book. I don't want to give examples or teach anyone anything, I am only trying to share a life full of experiences and photographs. For some photography will be nothing more than that moment kept in the past, for others it's simply a decorative object for the office or home, for me photography is a way to express your love for others.

This was an evolution, however. So although there was a time when I liked to photograph plants and flowers, that's passed now. At that time I thought it was important to share the beauty I could capture with my camera, but those that looked at it just saw a bee, a flower or a tree and did not see all the preparation that happens behind the image: the selection of the lens, the light and just the right moment to capture the image. For an untrained eye it was nothing more than a snapshot of nature, but for me there was beauty reflected in that photograph. As I mentioned though, it was only during a stage of my life that I later moved on from.

Now I think I am in a stage that we could call more

mature, because I learned that beauty is temporary and lost over time, and I also learned that beauty is personal and what one sees as beautiful the other person does not. You have to keep that in mind. I learned that beauty is only beauty but that there is much more behind it and more important things, hence I dedicated myself to portraiture. Although anyone may think that it is the same thing, only instead of doing it about flowers and plants it is about individuals, for me it is much more. It is about capturing the essence of the person, both what they do and do not want to share, since we are a set of desires, intentions and beliefs and I have specialised in this area for years. One may think that beliefs are universal and common to all, but when you move a few kilometres away you realise that the experience is totally different, even when sharing some beliefs, and it's expressed in a way of acting, dressing or celebrating differently. But if, instead of moving a few kilometres, we move a few hundred kilometres things change again. Since the same beliefs, customs and traditions aren't shared it can be at least a little surprising because of its differences. This is where I specialised after abandoning naturalistic photography.

Even though I do not consider myself an expert in religion or a theologian or anything like that, I am able to identify which society it is based on its' practices, and it's precisely these differences that I have tried to highlight in my photos, seeking to capture the moment and the essence of it. There are many anecdotes I could share, but maybe the events that called to me the most were linked to an introduction to someone changing religion, which is known as the conversion phenomenon. I don't know how to explain exactly why, but I think that it's one of the most emotional ceremonies, especially for the person experiencing it and their families. It's true that if we talk about emotional celebrations we can talk about weddings, in which two people promise to be happy together for the rest of their lives, or at least that is the initial intention. Another equally emotional moment, but in this case of an opposite feeling, would be funerals. But however emotionally charged these moments are, for me the most significant thing is the conversion. To someone else this phenomenon probably doesn't attract much attention, it's just about the transition between one belief or religion and another. But for me, abandoning what you believe in to adopt another belief, attracts my attention a lot because it's not only about a different religious practice, some new prayers or rituals, but leaving behind everything you thought before to adopt a new way of being and thinking. Maybe if we think about someone who didn't have a clear belief before, like in the case with atheists, we could believe or assume that the conversion is easier since they didn't have a belief before so adopting one is simpler than changing one you already have. A rather simplistic view of reality which does not correlate to what is happening: if a person did not have a belief before there is surely a reason. In the other case, of people who already have their own beliefs, maybe it's much easier to change to a new one so long as it offers something different to the previous. Therefore, it's about taking a step forward in personal development, so to speak. I suppose the reason for the change is looking for something different which is not found in the previous religion practised, although the motivations may depend upon each person. Whatever the individual story, for me the most emotional scenario was seeing this conversion ceremony.

Religions establish a calendar to comply with these celebrations throughout the year, to comply with practices which take place on certain dates. In some cases it's about remembering some past event which changed the course of history, or commemorating the birth or death of a prominent religious figure. Equally there are events throughout the year with celebrations linked to the moon, (because although they won't admit it, some religions were built on previous beliefs which meant admitting certain rites, even if they were adapted to new circumstances), as well as the arrival of spring or autumn because that's what was done before religion arrived. You would have to be a historian to know the origin of these ancestral customs though and I wasn't. I only tried to reflect what I could see, I sought to collect these rites and ceremonies and share them with others through my photography. My ambition was not to create a historical archive of customs at each place, as some editorials had suggested, but without looking for or wanting it at this stage of my life, this job allowed me to meet incredible people. It's not that they were different from the rest, or at least not in appearance, but their level of understanding of reality and human nature was far above what I could understand.

Sometimes these people were wise men, others were religious people, priests or similar, but in each case they had a great wisdom that I could not capture with my camera no matter how hard I tried. Primarily because they were not interested in portraying themselves for others, but also according to what they told me, they thought that I was wasting my time trying to transmit their teachings through an image. It was better that the person interested in learning their knowledge came to see them in person to listen or ask questions. This caused me a certain level of frustration at not being able to share their knowledge. Either way the photos did not turn out as I expected. It's not that they moved or tried to make it not come out the same, it's just that I couldn't capture that moment of wisdom. Despite that, focusing on portraying the celebrations and customs brought me many surprises, then quickly, when my work started to be recognised, different religious institutions started to call me to photograph their lives and rituals. It was something like a window into their world, to make themselves known. Despite that not being my initial intention, it seemed surprising that they now let me photograph practices that could not normally be seen, such as inside monasteries or convents which were normally reserved for initiates.

Although that was one of my most notorious stages in the world of photography, and it gave me some international prestige and renown, it's not what I dedicate myself to now. It's been a while since I stopped photographing religious leaders, festivities and celebrations in order to dedicate myself to portraying ordinary people. This could be unusual for people who think that power, fame and money are important, but for me, at this time of my life, the important thing is people independently of what they earn, what they dedicate themselves to and everything else. I'm not looking for exceptional people that wear different clothing or who have tattoos people haven't seen before. I dedicate myself solely and exclusively to photographing people who ask me to and

I make sure to ask for the contact details of a family member who could be contacted in the future so as to not repeat the unpleasant experience of my first job where I couldn't help that lady find her husband's picture. I don't know if that would help her with her loss or not but I spent a lot of time feeling uneasy thinking that someone had asked me for help and I hadn't been able to offer any. So every time I took one of these current photographs I asked for the contact details of a family member just in case they passed away. Equally, I ask them to give my business card to those family members so they would know that I will always have a copy of that person's picture, or at least, for as long as I'm alive. This was going to be my legacy for those that wanted it, and I don't know if it would ease the suffering of some widow but what's clear is that I was going to try to respond to a problem I couldn't solve at the time.

Despite the above, after my youth I had to learn that time takes everything away, even our memories, so some of the portraits I took were never claimed by anyone. Unlike that first woman I couldn't help, other people did not value the image of their loved one, or at least, did not value it in the same way. Sometimes because they didn't want to remember it when someone died, as in the case of that first woman; other times because they didn't realise that over time it would be the only thing left of their relatives. On some occasions I even proposed that they come and pick it up but they refused; particularly the ones who were sick or who were already a certain age, where the family preferred not to remember them that way, but the way they were when they were younger: they preferred to forget the last moments or years that were normally associated with the suffering of their loved one.

There are many anecdotes I could tell of that first job since I encountered new people every day and each with different interests. There were some who liked to talk and share things and others who came in for the photo and left. I had few memories of the latter whilst the former were more rewarding. Although the most important was the people like that first woman who wanted to… I don't know how to say it… recover time… or recover her husband or something. I'm not really sure what she was trying to do.

As a matter of fact, I wasn't in that first job very long. If I remember correctly, I didn't even last an academic year since the subjects were so demanding that in the end I decided to dedicate myself fully to studying despite the economic sacrifice it put on my parents. Doing the maths however, if I had to repeat that subject it would cost much more than I was earning in that job, so my experience in the world of work was cut off for years since I didn't start another job until I finished that degree. Maybe that's why that woman's decision to find her husband's pictures stayed with me so much. I never found it despite dedicating a few hours to it in secret when my boss wouldn't let me waste any more time. That woman was only looking for a photo of her husband, a photo of a face that no one remembered more than her, but a photo of such significance that she came to the door every day asking until she was asked not to return.

Something I learnt over time which was hard for me to accept was that we don't control our destiny, or at least not in the way we think. Although it's true that we can study or work to achieve our goals, what we achieve will not always correspond to the effort put in. At least that's what I had seen in my fellow students, both the ones who finished the degree and those who abandoned it, the intention and effort was one thing, but the achievement is quite another. Some say it's luck, others say that you need well connected acquaintances to get a job, but in my experience neither one nor the other guarantees the future. Without going into too much detail, I remember a colleague who, upon finishing his degree, began to teach at the university, and seemed to show promise for the academic world. I had already published several articles and collaborated on various investigations, but I was still looking for my first job. Well, my first job after finishing my degree because I already mentioned the experience I had in the world of photography.

Well, this colleague seemed to have a very promising future in the academic field following in the footsteps of his father who was a professor at the same university. If someone was rude, they could say that it was an arrangement that the father had made for the son to work at the same university, but I knew him as a student, I knew that he was an outstanding person who made a lot of effort to meet his father's expectations. That led him to have one of the best records in our class, so it didn't surprise me that he later stayed on as a university professor. So far so good for this colleague with a great record and future ahead of him. What no one could imagine was the sudden death of his father, and although he was starting college with a fairly moderate salary, it seems that this was not enough to cover the expenses that the family now had. Overnight he had become the household's money maker so he had to abandon his academic expectations and look for a higher paying job, only to find himself working in a bar. A surprise to anyone who knew his potential, but as he said: 'bills don't pay themselves and those first few years of academia pay very badly in comparison to other jobs.' So working in a bar he earned three times more than at the university; or at least that's what he told me when I happened to run into him on the street. Of course he would have wanted to go back to the university and finish up, but he was quite realistic and had his priorities clear, so he knew that things were not going to change overnight and he had to attend to the family's bills. An unexpected setback in life, but one that marked a person's future, disrupting dreams and plans. But, I have also met others who have had to change their life due to an unforeseen event. So, everything that matters to us is disrupted when for example, sickness appears, converting a useful person into a dependent one if it becomes serious and incapacitating and everything that has been fought for loses meaning with the only hope being able to recuperate lost health.

But I can talk about accidents as equally as illness. I remember in secondary school when someone came in in a wheelchair, a young person not much older than us. To begin with we didn't really know what she was doing there, but the teacher told us it was part of an awareness campaign about the importance of responsible driving to prevent traffic accidents. This person told us that before the accident she lived a more normal life, she had a partner and went to parties like any other girl her age, until one day while riding a motorcycle, which is how she got to school, she had the bad luck of being hit by a car not following zebra crossing rules at a roundabout, and that was the end of it. She stopped going out and studying and she had to go to a rehabilitation centre for months where she had to learn how to manage that chair. It's not that it was complicated, or at least that's what she told us, but she underwent several operations there until she was bedridden. She said she was not able to feel anything below the waist, but despite what doctors had said she was making progress every day. She was worried that it wouldn't happen fast enough, especially because she had lost her partner and her studies because of what happened. After that she hardly left her house until she spoke to a psychologist who apparently convinced her that life didn't end in a wheelchair.

That woman's testimonial was very emotive and made me think a lot about how brief everything in life is, and that it could end at any corner or roundabout, or at least that's how she described it. Maybe she was trying to teach us that we need to take care when we drive, but I came away with something different: something personal about how fleeting life is and the importance of finishing your studies. Someone could think that I had a mid-life crisis, so to speak, so much so that I requested a change of career, something my parents didn't really like at first, since they were hoping I would continue in the family business and help it to grow. But the testimony of this young girl in a wheelchair had made me wonder what was really important in life. It could be a profitable business, a big house and lots of possessions, but that won't help much if you lack good health. But what career would allow me to have good health? Maybe if you studied something related to physical activity or sport maybe you would be more aware of that part of life and you would be in better health. Maybe if you studied something linked to food like diet and nutrition, you would know how to feed yourself better and your health would improve over time. Of course, you could always study for a career in the health sector and then you could take care of yourself to the best of your ability.

That's why I abandoned the business career, something my parents had chosen arguing that it would help me in the future to achieve better economic performance when I was in charge of the family business, leaving it for something that seemed more promising to me at the time: psychiatry. It's not that I wanted to use it to solve people's problems per se, but rather I wanted to be prepared in case any of these unforeseen events occurred, since something had remained clear from the testimony of that young woman is that she had gone through great psychological suffering until she accepted her situation. So, reading between the lines, if we cannot control what happens to us in life, we can at least learn to manage how we experience it, so a career in psychiatry would help me to have greater psychological health in the face of what was in store for me in the future, be it good or bad. As I thought then, life can give you big surprises, but only for those who are unprepared. Unforeseen events can be experienced as something less negative, depending on how prepared you are psychologically, which is why I opted for a career in psychiatry. To begin with, my parents didn't understand my choice, especially because no one in the family had studied medicine before, but I was sure that this would prepare me for the trials of life and I could help others be healthier at the same time. Although I would have saved many more lives by choosing cardiac surgery, I preferred to think that mental surgery was equally as powerful as a scalpel, or perhaps more so. In fact, that young girl had told us that she had undergone several surgical interventions but in the end it was a psychiatrist that helped her move forward after she was discharged from hospital and had to face daily life.

That meant not only choosing a career but it implied several more years to specialise which caused my parents to complain since they believed in studies having a more immediate end, but in the end they understood that it was what I wanted. So after much thought they gave me their support: at least I was going to be a doctor with a specialism in psychiatry, so if I did not do well in psychiatry I could do another specialism and have more job opportunities. I accepted this reasoning, even though I didn't want to do anything beyond psychiatry. I did, however, later expand my field of research to include aspects of neuroscience, but that's another story. Within the world of psychiatry I specialised in discovering the person in front of me, of knowing them before they even spoke. So I could tell by looking at them if they angered easily, if they were suffering or if they were an affable person. You could think that this was some kind of magic trick, but it was just understanding their facial features since the most used muscles leave marks on the face. So, if someone angered quickly they would have forehead wrinkles from frowning often. On the other hand, if they were an affable and cheerful person, you would see pronounced dimples. This might sound strange but it's easier to understand if we think of a tennis player: surely they would have quite muscular arms or a swimmer would have a muscular back. Well, the same thing happens with the human face. If we use certain muscles in the face a lot when we show emotion, it will show. It's very useful for those of us that know how to read it: for me, it meant that I knew what type of person they were before they started talking.

I don't pretend to know more than the individual themself, but rather I could use it to know how to help them since in the field of mental health the most important thing is the person realising they need help. The next step is to teach them the techniques necessary to ensure that. But if that person is not capable of asking for help because they don't realise they need it or because they think it makes them seem weak, it is important to start working on those things first so that the therapy will be effective.

Over the years as a psychiatrist I tended to many types of patients, some with more difficult problems to treat than others, but if the person comes accompanied, the first question I would ask is who is accompanying you and why. This may seem trivial, but it was very important for me. If that person was 'forced' to come by this relative it would tell me that perhaps this patient would not be very cooperative. For example, in the case of children and young people, where parents bring them in to be treated without them knowing they have a problem and not wanting to change, it's a hint to the difficulties that would present themselves later when it came time for treatment. But I digress.

What I was saying is that I had specialised in learning the signs and symptoms of a person well before they started to talk. Specifically, recognising the features of the human face had become a useful tool as a way to access information they didn't want to tell me and also as a way to break the ice. At times patients, because in the end that's what they were, came with a certain reticence with respect to psychiatrists. I don't really know what that was based on, maybe motivated by this erroneous idea that mental health professionals were able to discover your most intimate secrets without you saying them aloud. I remember how one of my patients was a heavy smoker and confessed to me that he had tried to quit many times, using all the ways he knew. I suggested to him that he try a hypnosis clinic, and I don't really know why, but that man became very angry with me, arguing that for this he would have gone to the circus. Patiently, I had to explain that the hypnotherapist he would be referred to was a highly prestigious doctor who specialised in helping people with a smoking addiction and that was why I recommended he try it. But the patient complained, arguing that he didn't want to eat onions or cluck like a chicken, something I suppose he saw at a show since clinical hypnosis as a therapy has worked for many years and is even applied currently in surgical interventions, whether that's because the person themself asks for it or because they're allergic to the anaesthetic. An advance in science that the media has not reported, so it remained in collective imaginations as something from a circus. Whilst I received some formal training on it, I did not consider myself an expert, so whenever I had a case where I thought it would come in handy I referred them to this colleague. Personally I believe that if a therapy will make a patient better, and if it's one that I am not proficient in, then it's better if another professional takes over and applies it for the good it can offer the patient.

Maybe the topic of the mind is an easier question to discuss on the part of patients than other medical topics, so if your doctor told you that you needed a heart bypass or surgery no one would discuss if that's the best technique for you. But on the other hand, if this doctor commented, like in this case, that you need a clinical hypnosis, everyone seems to know or have an opinion on if that's the best thing or not. I've had many years of professional practice where someone says what is the best or worst for them, especially when someone that isn't trained in psychological therapies. In some countries psychiatric attention is a basic service offered by health insurance; no one would think about taking out medical insurance that doesn't cover it. But in my country it's a luxury item, only available to those who can pay for it. Certainly a big health system error since it would save a good part of patient consultations because it's known that some people, whether because they are alone or because they've got nothing better to do, go to health services taking up professionals time and resources when they could be caring for people who need it more. I don't want to minimise these people's need for attention and care, but unlike other patients their situation is not so urgent, and I am not just referring to Munchausen syndrome, where a person makes a true pilgrimage to all the assistance centres, doing all kinds of tests to see if you discover a disease that you never have. Although hypochondria is the exaggerated fear about one's own health, Munchausen syndrome goes a little further, since it's not a worry about having an illness but a patient is aware that nothing is wrong with them but still goes to health services to be seen. In fact, after multiple tests and possible pathological possibilities have been dismissed, when the patient is confronted with their problem (or not as the case may be), there are occasions where the patient disappears and begins the process again at another facility looking for the same attention. Several of these patients have come to me for consultation, although not willingly: they were normally referred by these care centres because they saw that they didn't appear to improve despite being treated. Personally, and as a psychiatrist, that was a great challenge for me because there are a lot of secondary benefits for them, like the patient getting what they wanted: attention from a specialist to determine if they have an illness. The greater the need for this benefit, the more difficult it will be to cure this person. For example: if a patient was spending three to five days a week in a hospital centre to see what was wrong with them, they will not want to lose your attention which will impede their treatment.

But anyway, I'm getting away from the part of my life that I want to share. Let's see... where was I.... Although my first experience of the world of photography was at the start of my career, it was almost forgotten about since several years passed before I returned to work in the industry. So when I started as a consultant I applied all the techniques I had learned and developed during my career, but... I don't know how to say it... over time everything drifted until I became a specialist in the human face, which allowed me to know if that person was lying or telling the truth, and if they were willing to change or were forced to be there. I mean forced in the most literal sense of the word, since some patients were forced to come by the company they worked for, whilst others were forced by their partner as a way to solve their problems before ending the relationship. Of course, being forced to come to therapy is almost a guarantee that it will not work, since the person has to voluntarily work to improve themself: they have to be convinced that it's beneficial for them.

But anyway, returning to the analysis of the face, we know that each one is different, but we should not lose sight of the fact that there are two elements to this: genetic and environmental. Yes it's true that our face develops in a skull which is genetically established, but the muscles we use are going to configure it too, that's to say, we can know who our parents are, but we can also know who and how we are. I've said this in a very succinct way since there are many years of study and investigation behind it, so much so that sometimes the police have asked for my services. In these cases it was about presenting me with some faces created via a machine, that is, portraits based on a witness testimony about a criminal they were looking for. This collaboration, although it happened on occasion, was not very frequent. The police wanted me to say who the criminal was based on the portrait, but it doesn't work like that, especially since a witness doesn't usually focus on fundamental details needed to analyse the human face. Testimonies normally talk about the colour of skin, hair or even eyes, if they had any scars, or even what their eyebrows were like. But they often forget the most important things for me, the form of the facial muscles which reflect the most used ones. As I say, that can only be told by a trained eye, so my help to the police was quite limited. Which is why, if they'd given me a proper machine portrait, I could say much more about the person they were looking for, but with what they normally showed me I could hardly give any relevant data. But clearly, one cannot ask the witnesses for more, it's a lot that they were able to remember details about the person in that moment, and of course the police do a lot with the little information that can be provided.

CHAPTER 2. THE BACK OF THE PICTURES

The old photograph appeared one day,
Someone had forgotten it: left it in a drawer.

A smiling man, looking dreamy
captured by the photographer.

He looked happy, young and attractive.
Immortalised in the photo.

No one knows who he is, there is no information
on him or who took the photo.

The old photograph is well preserved;
You can see it in the shiny face of that young man.

He should have stayed in photography.
You can still see it,

With his shirt buttoned up and his sleeves rolled up,
With his baggy trousers and his hands outstretched.

What did he ask for? What did he want? No one will ever
know.
Only the photograph: leaving us to wonder.

We cannot find any memories or news of him.

Did he live here? Surely, no one remembers.

Was he in love?

Maybe it was a photo given to his beloved, to a woman.

She kept it safe in a drawer,

And didn't tell anyone, because it was a test of love,

Sent by her lover, maybe he was far away,

Maybe by looking at the picture she didn't forget him.

But time is unyielding, it goes by without stopping,

What happened to the woman? No one knows.

All you can see is the photograph,

Forgotten in a drawer, where it was yesterday.

Maybe it was a distant yesterday, a past farther back

than a picture in hand,

A picture of who? No one will ever know.

LOVE

It took me some time to understand the importance of, and to put in place, writing on the back of the picture the story of who was in it. At first I was young and didn't think that type of annotation would be necessary, but with time I realised that my memory was not as good as I thought. Maybe it was time or maybe it was the number of photos I accumulated year after year, since at least once a month I tried to take a portrait of someone I considered special, someone I came across and connected with. Had I started this past time any earlier I surely would have included one of my teachers in the list of memories, or even loved ones that had died of old age before I got to really know them: my grandparents. Although since school I've had a certain predilection for teachers: trying to learn more from them than the subject they taught. Considering them to be elderly wisemen capable of sharing the meaning of life. Later there then came people who were not so academically outstanding who taught me selflessly. In the end I realised that you could learn from anyone in any situation without waiting for them to become a great scholar. In a way the words of people I crossed paths with were guiding me or helping me in some way. I don't mean that I was hoping for some kind of sign or indication to know what to do each day. I mean that in the moments where I needed help it came in the form of a response someone was giving and it was very good for me.

But getting back on track, human memory is fragile and even though it's strong in your youth, it starts to weaken: losing itself little by little. Even in the more important situations, where to begin with we record every detail, whether it's a wedding or the birth of our first child, or even the first time we kiss someone, all those moments we remember well: over time they start to blur. That's why I started to write the information on the back of the photo, so I wouldn't forget: the day it was taken, the name of the person, their job and why they had the picture taken. For example, there was an older woman who stood out to me: "she taught me not to expect others to behave as I want them to", or the sailor on whose picture I wrote: "he goes out every day to see what life brings him and he does it with such joy"... so many photographs, and each one of them a reflection, a thought, a moment of learning. But there came a time when I stopped taking photographs, I had lost the meaning of it, and I didn't know what to do with the ones I had on the wall. It was a sad period in my life, when I had some continuing losses and needed some time to get over them. Back then, my passion had taken a back seat, I no longer had any intention of looking at it. Perhaps that was when I needed more help, but back then I didn't even look at them.

I don't know if everyone has that moment in their life, a sort of existential crisis so to speak, where you wonder if what you are doing really matters or not. It could be that over time people don't even think about it, so they become accustomed to doing the same thing every day. It could be that they forget why they do it, and continue to for the rest of their life. But sometimes, there are events which make you wonder if you are really doing something you like or something that fulfils you, although sometimes this event is not pleasant. At least that's what happened in my case, where two of the people I loved the most, my parents, died close together.

My father was the first to pass away, but my mother didn't last a year being without him, and as some say she died of grief; something I didn't notice. Had I been able to realise this I would have gotten my mother professional help, but at the time I was also in mourning so I didn't see the situation with the emotional distance it needed. I justified some of my mothers actions that, looking back now, were indicative that something was wrong. I'm not saying that she was depressed, or maybe I am, I don't know. What was clear is that the loss of her husband, to whom she had been married 30 years, was a big emotional blow that she did not recover from. I was a mental health professional and I should have recognised the symptoms.

Symptoms that I detected daily in my patients which allowed me to know if I should prescribe them medicine to help them deal with their situation. But with my mother I didn't, or couldn't, detect it nor intervene early enough and it wasn't long after she died that I realised what had happened.

It was after this second loss that I had one of my worst moments, where I wanted to be away from everything, including my profession, to grieve, so I looked for a quiet place close to nature and I went to live there indefinitely. The idea was to have my space, a place where I could take long walks by the river, where I didn't have to worry about patients coming to see me with their own problems, and where I was far away from painful memories of loss. I knew that it was a temporary arrangement, at some point I would have to go back and confront the situation, go back to my daily activity of answering questions in my office, but at that moment I was enjoying a well deserved vacation, if you can call it that.

The truth is that I had not even thought about how long it was for, only that I needed to get away from everyone and everything. So I found a pretty place far from the city, where mobile phone coverage was bad which allowed me to not be hanging onto a phone that barely worked. I don't know how it happened, but in nature those injuries healed little by little, or at least, they didn't hurt as much. On my walks I noticed that the morning dew gave way to an impressive sun at midday until it cooled at night when you could see the stars. It was in this peace that I returned to thinking about photographs, and how no one would care what they reflected. But for me, it was important that in some way the image remained of that person who, for a moment, had been my life teacher, and that their reflection or phrase be jotted down along with their name. If someone took all those photographs they could surely write a self-help book full of deep phrases to reflect on; or that's how it seemed to me anyway. Maybe in time I will even decide to write that book myself, and I will not try to recount the life of each person I met and photographed, but simply write the phrase and comment on it, indicating the meaning that I took from it in case someone gets help when they needed it. I suppose it will be difficult for that phrase to reach someone just when they need it, but at least all the teachings I have collected in my life will be there.

Maybe without realising it, we go through life doing what we think is the most important thing in each moment and then... the truth is that if you look at it with perspective, it wasn't so important after all. It's true that many things we do serve us well in the future, but over time you realise that the important thing is not what you achieve or what you have but who you shared the time with; or at least that was my experience. In my long work as a therapist I was able to see patients of different ages and the older ones all talked about the same thing, the amount of time they dedicated to pretending or achieving and how they regret not having dedicated that time to their loved ones, who were either alone far away or had died. That's to say, there was a time of coexistence that could not be recovered. Personally, I liked it: listening to the person to attend to their needs, trying to learn their experiences, to enrich myself as much as possible. Although each one has their own life experience based on the unique and unrepeatable circumstances they go through, that doesn't mean you can't learn from others. This, together with my desire to leave a record of people that have positively influenced my life, had led to my collection of photographs which I showed to everyone who came to my house, although it was not always well understood. I suppose it must be the sight of so many different photos on the wall, there were maybe a hundred, I don't know what the guests thought, but sometimes they were afraid and sometimes they disapproved. It could be that they thought it was some kind of obsession, like the people motivated by paranoia who look for connections where there aren't any; a clear sign of someone with mental health issues like those I have met. I know the symptoms and social and personal consequences that these obsessions entail, but it wasn't like that for me: it was just a hobby that had gradually become a wall full of photos that I added to occasionally. I continued it, wanting to leave a message of hope, but also a memory of someone who went through life contributing their grain of sand to the world.

Personally, I didn't consider one life more valuable than another, even though sometimes politicians, artists or scientists may seem more valuable or more important since they leave their name in the history books. That wasn't the sort of memory I wanted to keep, since there were other people dedicated to that. My aspirations were simple: it was my intention that this person and his life be remembered, famous or not.

But well, just like I said about that time I almost gave up this hobby, I've had ups and downs, maybe because I didn't meet anyone I considered remarkable, or maybe at the time I wasn't receptive to what they told me. Whatever it was, there were several periods where I have gone months and even years without adding a new photograph to my collection. But for me that was important, because whenever I needed it, when I couldn't find an answer to a problem that was posed to me, I stood in front of those photographs and contemplated them for hours. I don't know how it happened, but one of them caught my attention. It's not that it was different from the rest, it just seemed strangely striking to me, and despite continuing to look at the rest of the photographs, I kept coming back to that one until I finally decided to pick it up to look at it carefully. I then remembered who this person was, more or less the circumstances in which I had known them and, the most important thing, what they had given me, all that information logged on the back of the photo. But strangely for me that small phrase, which was sometimes no more than five words, was precisely what I needed in those moments where I couldn't find a solution to my problem. I don't know how it was possible, but there was a phrase behind every picture, a teaching, a response, and it was exactly what I needed at that moment.

Whilst you could think that all the world's knowledge doesn't fit in a single phrase, if we think about the words of great philosophers, presidents or other famous people in history: it's sometimes only one or two phrases we remember. No matter how many discussions they have, apart from a few phrases no one remembers them. But those sentences are their essence, so to speak, what distinguishes them from others and what they contribute to history. Sometimes they were lucky phrases: they inspired change in a whole generation. Others were unlucky phrases: unexpected or inappropriate but stuck in the annals of history due to the relevance of the person who said them.

Be that as it may, there are only a few phrases which make a person famous, and in my case, I did the same: pick up a teaching, a thought or a phrase which, I don't know how to word it... resonated within me when I met that person. Each and every one of those photographs were of people I've met and who I have learnt an important lesson from. It doesn't matter to me if that person is famous, a scholar or someone with a modest job; if something they say resonates in me then I try to leave it behind in my photography. Over time the collection of teachings became so big that it surprised me to see how easy it had been to collect, how I had accumulated such knowledge found in the world. I don't know if people realised what they knew, that they were able to give a response to the questions in their life. To realise that they would have to stop a bit and think of the problem and then find the answer. But as strange as it may seem, and even having an answer for someone else, people sometimes don't find an answer to their own problems because they don't deviate from their daily rhythm: they continue their hectic lives, sometimes for years, with this unresolved problem. It's something strange, to see how people are capable of expertly advising others whilst not finding a solution to their own problems, despite how obvious the solution may seem from the outside. It may be that at times we are so stubborn we don't find a solution to our problems, that we stop trying to find another way. Instead, from the outside, the solution is so obvious that others, knowing your problem, can offer you a correct answer. From there, the second problem is not being open to what others can teach you, that is, if they offer you the solution to the problem you have, you only have to accept it, and then you can solve it. Something which seems so obvious requires a lot of humility to know that others can help you and teach you about what you have not been able to solve on your own.

Well, in this regard I would like to share what happened to me one day when that small woman accompanied me home.

"What is your favourite message?" Asked the woman to whom I was showing my collection. It was on rare occasions that I invited someone to visit my photography collection. I don't know why, but I felt a connection to this person, as though I could confide my secret in her. Strangely, that woman not only didn't take it badly, but was pleasantly surprised and that's why I wanted her to see the collection once I had explained its purpose. She was there for a while looking at each photo, but until that moment she had not said anything, and I had already shown her some of the messages that were on the back.

"I don't know, maybe this one," I indicated the photo of an old man that I had met in Milan airport. He was an older man who told me he used to travel once a year to reunite with his family and he felt that this would be his last year. Despite that he wished for his loved ones to have a good life and hoped that he left them with good memories. It was a sad story in which his wife had passed away years ago so he was practically alone in life. But he bit the bullet and made those trips across the pond to be with his family for a few days. This way he could see his children, grandchildren and even great-grandchildren; a big family for sure. The only problem, or at least that's what he told me, was that as a young man his relatives moved far away and so he could only see them once a year.

The curious woman picked up a photo and turned around. With a smile she said:"I like it!" indicating the message on the back of the photo which said: 'live one day at a time'.

After putting it on the table, where I had put them for easier reach, she was looking at others until she said: "And this one?" showing me a picture of a little girl.

"This one is also very special, it's my niece, my sister's daughter. Well, her eldest daughter; she has since had two more children: a boy and a girl. Well, from her I have learnt to have dreams. She has always had them, and since she was small she thought that you could get anything just by wanting it, that you only had to wish really hard and then what you wanted would happen."

"Clearly, that's how children think." she said, taking it from me to look at.

"Yes of course, but she said it with such energy and vitality that I forgot all my problems stood beside her."

"Give life a chance." she read from the back of my niece's picture.

"Yes, I know it's very simple, but for me it contains a great message: innocent but also optimistic and that's why I kept it in my collection."

This was the most gratifying of all, when I could share something. I spent my whole life collecting snippets of memory: images and phrases from others that I didn't want forgotten, and I tried to share it with people who understood its value. I didn't want anyone to learn everything I had collected, nor did I want them to find a phrase that would change their life, I only wanted to share something that had served me well in case it could do the same for another.

Before the woman left I asked her if she would be willing to be part of my collection, if she would let me photograph her and collect a sentence from her. After much hesitation she said: "But I am not famous, and I don't think that I could say anything like those you have already collected."

"That doesn't matter," I commented, "everyone has something to teach in a certain moment, you just have to learn to listen."

"Oh really? So in my case what would you put?"

"Let me think… 'live with curiosity.' I think that defines you."

"I like that a lot. I will let you take my picture and you can put that phrase on it."

So I did. I moved her to a side room where I had a stool with a blank background behind it, and a camera on a tripod. I turned off the lights to avoid shadows and asked her to smile. She did and I took the picture which formed part of my archive of knowledge that I could call upon.

To tell the truth, I had really improved my photography skills since the first photos I took anywhere with no thought to the lighting which sometimes meant that the person didn't look good. They were kept in my collection not for the artistic image but for the phrase that person had given me.

I had met that woman in a supermarket and I don't know why but she started talking to me about her older children. One of them was in the army and she was worried about him. That conversation continued into the cafeteria where she told me details about her life and her youth and how she wanted to be a professional ballerina. She had barely made it through the first rehearsals before being rejected. That frustration didn't stop her from being involved in the world of music and dance though. So much so that she had managed to develop a method for her little ones to learn to read. At first it didn't have much of a place in her current profession as a teacher, in which she cared for children between the ages of three and six, because many times the parents only expected her to have their children there while they worked. But she was not satisfied and intended for her children, as she liked to call them, to also acquire skills related to reading, or at least that was her effort for years until she discovered that she could do it through dance and music. In principle the method appeared simple, she gave each child a letter and an associated ballet movement so that when they started to read each one had to act out and dance each letter. It was something very simple, or at least that's what she thought, but surprisingly the children learned very quickly, even quicker than others their age who hadn't done this game. So this teacher became an example for other teachers as a way to strengthen reading habits amongst students from their first words. All this she told me in the cafeteria and, surprised, I asked her the motive behind this, how this had occurred to her and she told me that it was due to a curiosity she had had since childhood and thanks to that she tried to improve on everything she did, and this was the case in the educating of young people.

Those are the people whose lives and experiences I like to share, when someone turns to my photography corner where I have portraits of everyone and everything, that's to say, the sentence is maybe an excuse to hear that person's life, or at least the part that I knew and which called to me. It wasn't about telling that person's biography because everyone will have had both good and bad moments. The important thing for me was to show people who have had a positive impact on others. Sometimes it was about little movements and changes, other times it was about their big impact on others, but they all shared a spirit of improvement that guided them. Nowadays for example they can be compared to heroes; to those who willingly or unintentionally leave their mark on the history of a place or at least on a few lives. That would be something like those photos, portraits of my heroes, those who were able to impact me in a positive way for a moment through their words or their example.

But maybe the most important of all was not only that

I had an ever growing collection of photos, but the surprising thing is those people I showed it to and explained the reasons behind it, tended to replicate it: to look for their own heroes. I don't know why. It's not that they were going to make their own collection of hero portraits, but they were able to learn from people they crossed paths with and were ready to learn from each situation, but without forcing it, just leaving it to flow only when you felt it and accepting it into your life. It was a new experience, but a marvellous one. At least, that's what people told me when they managed it: incorporating into their lives this capacity to be amazed and to learn from each person they made contact with. That means, at least for me, that everyday and everywhere there are heroes who can teach us a lot if we are willing to learn. On occasions it's dedication and certainty; other times it's love for another or to have dreams... so many teachings that I have been able to experience, which surely would have been different for other people, but were rewarding all the same. The person has to give themselves over to the opportunity for it to happen, without doing anything: without forcing it. Just have curious eyes, like children who are amazed by everything: even the simplest thing like a falling leaf or the leisurely walk of a snail.

57

CHAPTER 3. PHOTOGRAPHY SCHOOL.

There are moments in life, where you have
to stop a little and decide where to go.

Some decisions are more important: you have to reflect,
ask opinions then choose or reject.

When you go on a bicycle and, hesitating, you stop
Where am I going now? You think a bit.

Time passes, you have grown now, you have to decide
Whether to study this or that.

You chose a career, follow it with effort
That first illusion: I have made it, I have done it.

The moment arrives, when you have to decide
Will you stay in your city, or go elsewhere?

Maybe you will have more work opportunities
If you move there, if you leave everyone behind.

Life decisions, difficult to make
But there is no other solution, you have to continue.

This person that you look at, it seems like they like you
You are older now, sensible, and you believe you are
ready.

After a lot of thinking, the decision you have made
you've asked them and it's time to get married.
A difficult decision, and it cost you a lot,
but you said yes and you liked it.

Throughout life you have to make decisions
For you, or at work, they happen all the time.

Some are very simple, like choosing food
The suit I wear today, or postponing an outing.

But others, however, we are forced to make.
It costs what it costs, but we have to give a response.

Faced with such difficulty, today we have to think.
They await the decision that we are going to make.

LOVE

Although at first I rejected the idea of doing a kind of photography school, over time I realised that it could be something useful and necessary. I'm not talking about a school where you only teach about different bits of equipment, or how to choose the right lens or filter to apply a certain technique; there are older and more experienced people than me for that job. I would try to teach how to capture the essence of a person, their soul in a broad sense of the word, in fact, I discovered this meaning on a trip.

I have travelled to different continents in my life and tried to capture the moments I considered the most beautiful, dedicating special attention to photographing the habits and customs of the people that live there: their clothes, gestures or festivities. Surprisingly, I found myself in various countries that had a philosophy when it came to photography where they didn't want or didn't like to be photographed. For example, the orthodox jewish community feel uncomfortable when someone looks at them strangely or photographs them. One theory could be a sort of personal or cultural mistrust, but it falls short when compared to what I found in other places. So, in India some people believed that photography captured a person's soul and not everyone was willing to let that happen. Equally, there are places in Australia where aborigines don't always want you to take photographs. At first, I attributed this idea to a chance personal mistrust or even a lack of culture, since photography is nothing more or less than capturing a reflection of the moment, but in no case does it ever capture more of the person than their image. Overtime I understood that the lack of culture was mine, and despite the hundreds of thousands of photographs I had taken, I had not been aware of what I was doing. In each of those photographs I had effectively captured the moment, but I had also captured the person's landscape, furniture or clothing. Without a doubt, they are a great memory of the places I had been, they helped me to see where I had gone, almost as if I had bought one of the many postcards that are sold at airport kiosks. But apart from that I also photographed people and they were unique and incomparable people through their character, their way of thinking and their actions. Bearing in mind that behind this image is a whole vital history of that individual that has born, grown, developed and arrived at the moment I had taken their picture, in a way they are always alive in that image, even if years have passed since their death. To think that some people believe that a person is born, develops and dies and then a memory is all we have of them; some cultures believe that we only live in that moment and when we die that person ceases to exist. Although there are more spiritual people who justify it by not giving importance to the body and instead focusing on a person's essence which can even be transferred to other bodies. Quite different to the ways and cultures I have become accustomed to, but of course I had to learn them and respect them.

The first time was quite shocking: when I was going to take a picture and an Orthodox Jew covered his face with the hat he was wearing. I took the photograph, although of course all his clothes came out except his face. On another occasion I took a trip to Australia to photograph an aborigini, and when he saw what I was going to do he turned around so that I could only see his back, so I didn't even bother taking the picture.

I also have this one anecdote that I still don't know how to explain. It's about a man, who wasn't even that old, whom I had been told was special, something akin to a healer for people who had exhausted traditional medicine and still couldn't find a solution to their problem. "People like this are very desperate and try every method which gives them a little hope". At least, that's what I thought at the time, and with curiosity I tried to approach this man to try and photograph him. So for several days I tried to discover where I could find this man but it seemed to be a jealously guarded secret in the town I was visiting. At the time the reason for this was unknown, but I was tipped off that people didn't like the fact that he didn't charge for his services, so once they had called the healer, he didn't charge them anything: not his loved ones nor other sick people. Very commendable, but people living off that business and other peoples desperation didn't like it. I found out later that there had been several attempts on his life, without success, but that was why he was so hard to find by people who were not in dire need. But, one day they finally told me where I could find him and directed me to his house, after interrogating me about my intentions. Once I arrived, an old woman with a big smile opened the door and invited me for a drink whilst we awaited the healer. It seemed strange to me but I accepted, and whilst having a drink I got to know the man next to me who was also having one. We were sat in the hallway drinking peacefully and conversation started:

"How long have you been waiting?"

"I just got here," I said, surprised by the question.

"Well I've been here for a few hours, although I have been away from duty."

"Oh I didn't know it took so long."

"No idea, I only know that still no one has attended me."

"Well, have you seen any others?"

"Yes, before me I saw a woman who came alone and

another woman with her son. Both of them were here for a few hours and then they left."

"Where did they go?" I asked, curious.

"Apparently they go through those curtains." He indicated the green ones at the back of the room.

Instinctively, I got up to move closer to that place to see if I could see anything, but the old woman came through the door beside me and told me to sit down and that she would tell me when someone had come by. Somewhat frustrated by that, I didn't want to spend hours sat down just to take a picture, I tried to get the most information possible and leave; at least I would have a good story even if I didn't get a picture, so I asked the man who had kindly shared a drink with me.

"Well, you don't look sick," I commented somewhat insidiously.

"Not all illnesses can be seen on the outside." He lifted the cup to his mouth to drink a little.

"And how good is this healer?" I asked.

"Healer? You must have made a mistake."

"It's not the healer's house?"

"No, there's a restorer here" he sipped his drink again.

"Healer, restorer, what difference is there, as long as they cure illness?"

"There isn't one really, like you say, as long as they cure

illness." He commented with a slight smile.

That annoyed me a little since I didn't know if he was wasting my time. If this person was in front of me and each one took hours to attend to, it could be that I wouldn't be seen until the afternoon. I looked at the clock and said, like someone who doesn't want something:

"Are you in a hurry?"

"For what?" He asked, surprised.

"To be attended to." I asked, revealing my intentions.

"Not really, you can go in front of me if you want." He commented, smiling.

That's what I wanted, saving myself from spending hours sitting there doing nothing but drinking a little, however tasty it might be.

After a few moments, and reflecting on what he was doing there, I thought that if that man was sitting there it could be that he had one of those illnesses that science couldn't explain, maybe a cancer which couldn't be seen externally... it seemed insensitive of me to inquire about something so personal, but what was clear is that he was there because he needed it but me... Whilst thinking on this, the old woman came in and asked me to come through, which surprised me since I had already become accustomed to the idea that I would spend hours sat there, but now I had the opportunity to meet this healer. I got up from the chair and went to go behind the curtain, but stopped, turned and said:

"No, it's better if this man goes first, I'm not in any real hurry." I turned back to my seat with resignation.

"It's your turn." Insisted the old woman, stopping me with a gentle hand and guiding me back towards the green curtain. Curious, I pushed it open and didn't see anything special. Just a room similar to this one with two chairs at the end of the room, one in front of the other. There was no one there. The old woman who had accompanied me inside said:

"Sit down for a moment, and he will be here." She then left through that same green curtain. I did as she asked, looking all around, although the truth is that there wasn't much to see: only the walls and a light on the ceiling. Suddenly, the man I was sat with appeared through the curtain and said:

"Nothing is wrong with you, why have you come?"

That surprised me because we were no longer in the waiting room, but in a consulting room, or something like it. But to my surprise he sat down in the other empty chair that was in front of me, and at that moment I realised.

"You're the healer… well, restorer?" I asked, surprised.

"Yes, I am." He confirmed with a smile.

"You told me you were ill." I protested.

"I said that some illnesses can't be seen from the outside." He corrected me.

"Well yes, maybe… anyway, I want to take a photo." I asked, not wasting time.

"You don't want to know how I do it?"

"Do what?" I asked, curious.

"Well restore people's health."

"I don't know if I would understand it, I just came to take a photo of you." I insisted.

"Very well, then take it, I give you my permission."

So I stood up and moved a little so that I could get better light. After taking it I sat down again and said: "Thank you, everything seemed a little strange to me, starting from when you didn't introduce yourself in the other room."

"Don't you want to write the phrase down?"

"What phrase?" I asked, surprised.

"The one you put on the back of each photo."

"Ah yes, tell me, I don't have a good memory."

"The destiny isn't what's important, what's important is that you are happy on the journey."

"That's it? That's all?" I asked, waiting for a proverb or sentence with a dual meaning.

"That's it. If you apply this to your life, you will see how everything changes."

"But is it like a reflection, a life lesson, what is it?"

"It's just a sentence, one of those you put on the back of each photo."

"How did you know that?" I asked, surprised because only a few close family members had seen my collection.

"It's part of my job, getting to know the person I am trying to get back on track."

"What track are you talking about? I asked, now surprised by that enigmatic phrase.

"Each of us has a path, marked for us by our Creator and it depends on us to live it in one way or another. There are those who insist on fighting against their path, trying to change it, but in reality it only fills their life with frustration. Others, on the other hand, learn to accept it and to work in favour of others."

The conversation was getting increasingly more strange, and I didn't know if I wanted to go deeper into what it was about, because I had only gone to take this person's photo and it seemed that I was there longer than expected. It's true that on occasion people tried to tell me something they understood to be the truth. Later it turned out that each one had their own truth. Anyway, that day I left with a photo and a sentence I wrote down so I wouldn't forget.

The problem is that when I went to develop the photo

it came out blank. Well, not exactly blank... I don't know how to describe it... the person didn't appear in the photo and there was a blank, illuminated space where he should be. The rest of the photo came out okay, not blurred or out of focus, you could even see the green curtains and the light, but no people. To begin with I put it down to a camera error, or something; I didn't know how to explain it. In the end I accepted that this was the photo of him, I came to imagine him as a man without a face and to this day his message is an enigma: how he knew about me and what I was doing but especially how he knew to say those words I needed at that moment to be able to change my life.

Well, from my way of thinking now, you can live life in two ways. The first is what the majority of people do: live to work, charged with debts to pay not knowing if they would make it to the end of the month. The other is much simpler and is about accepting what life gives you, without question, whether good or bad. Simply go forward in life without worrying about tomorrow; knowing that our destiny isn't in our hands, but the path we follow and the life we live is. If we worry, anguish and stress about it, it is us affecting our lives in an insane way that makes us sick. But, if we choose tranquillity and positive thinking, we can appreciate life and take greater advantage of it rather than living just to live without any greater meaning. I learned all this thanks to that visit, where something was not physically healed or restored in me because I was not sick, but something inside me changed my way of seeing the world. I no longer wanted to be a mere spectator of my own life, I wanted to take control of it: not to achieve my goals and objectives, but to accept what was presented, trying to see the positive in it whether I understood it or not.

So, this dream I had to create my own photography school teaching something, I don't know what to call it, philosophy on life linked with the art of photography. It was my initial intention and at the start I believed that it was a great idea, but over time I deflated: going back to my daily work where I worried more about paying bills from month to month than about carrying out altruistic plans and projects.   It's true that I had shared my worries with other people, and one person had even encouraged me to do it and generously offered me a place where I could deliver classes. Despite having prepared posters advertising the course, in the end I didn't start it. I don't know if people were prepared for what I wanted to share, or maybe it was me that wasn't sure it was a good idea. Until now I had shared an affinity for photography and what I had learnt with few people, the teaching of it, I don't know, it seemed more complicated.

I don't know how to explain it, but it was hard for me

to start, thinking it was a waste of time for myself and others. Thinking about it, I understood that the path has to be carved out for everyone personally, and just as it had happened to me, their answers would arrive in time. Even if I tried to teach what to look for in others or even simply to accept what others transmit to you, I don't know if it would be enough. I didn't want that meeting to turn into a session where I recounted my life or that of each of the photographs; I preferred to do that in private, with people who I believed would be able to take advantage of what they could communicate. Furthermore, in my life business has not gone well, the greatest achievements were produced when I personally expended the effort. The rest, no matter what I did, once it was left in someone else's hands it didn't turn out as expected.

73

CHAPTER 4. THE PERFECT MOMENT

Years fly by, the last day arrived
without me noticing, it seems like it never existed.

No memories left of time gone by
Maybe there were happy days, maybe I had some.

Where has the time gone? I don't know, quickly it trickles
away
Like water in your hands, it's gone, escaped.

Or this puddle on the ground the rain has made,
The sun hits it hard and it dries right away.

So time passed, day after day never stopping
It runs away, no remedy.

Past memories quickly forgotten
enjoyable days gone forever.

Maybe I took holidays or stayed at home,
Oblivion arrived, I don't remember.

Life goes by fast, never stopping
Even if you want it to, you will have to endure.

Living with enthusiasm is one thing,
But remembering it after, costs a lot.

What did I do in January? Impossible, it ended
So did February and March; everything is gone.
Maybe I remember August, a good time
had on the beach, or was it not that month?

Yes, mauve coloured in spring, I turned around
Soaked through with rain. Or not?

I'm sure of one thing, that it was cold in winter
And maybe we took a walk in the snow.

They are imprecise memories, that I will also forget
Memory is a problem needing a solution.

I don't drive anymore, I get lost.
Right and left are the same to me.

What happened to my life? It wasn't like this before
Memories are gone and I don't know what I did.

Memory, my memory, where are you? Why are you gone?
You left a hole behind, not knowing what I lived through.

If I went to the river or the mountain, if I ate or slept
Without memories I don't know what the year was like.

New Years Eve how fast you arrived!
How life is spent! It's almost over.

Was I happy? I don't know. What did I do? I don't
remember
Only that I am here, that I still know.

I must have had knowledge because I can still write
But how did I learn that? The memory is gone, I don't
remember.

Maybe I had a family, someone who accompanied me
Now I am alone, everything is forgotten.

There are many photos glued on the walls
I don't remember who they are though, smiling back at
me.

Memory has gone, I don't know where or why
What did I do wrong, what did I drink, maybe that's why
it left.

Like the year ends, I have almost ended
without memory, without memories of the past.

How can I survive, I can't walk anymore
It's impossible to leave: I fear not returning.

Where am I going? What have I come in here for?
Hard to answer when you have no memory, life comes to
an end.

Maybe you'll hang on for a long time, or maybe one more
day
But you don't enjoy it because you're going to forget it.

But there is still time to live and enjoy
All those who love you and who are by your side.

It doesn't matter to you that a tomorrow will come,
A new year starts, it's just another day.

Await with happiness, what life gives you
Memories or not, make others happy.

Maybe one day you forget it, this will not be important
You show them your affection, they won't forget it.

"New year, new me" the same refrain is always said,
Your new resolution, will it be fulfilled?

Jot down in the book you always have to hand,
The important things you don't want to forget.

Sit in front of the TV that you watch everyday,
Notebook in sight, so you don't forget.

Put down your name and address, anything you want to
remember,
Maybe there is a long way to go, when you won't even be
able to read.

Try not to be alone, talk to others,
Solitude isn't good, it doesn't help.

And if you are reading this, and something has helped
Smile, thinking it's not happened to you yet.

But to someone you know, maybe you have noticed
memory problems, and you scolded them.

Think about how you feel, when you have lost something
Glasses or an earring, and then it appeared.

But he is losing something that won't come back
A lifetime of memories, and he won't get them back.

Understand his situation and try to help him
Show him all your love, maybe he'll remember.

It's life, there's no solution, you can't avoid it
You can't stop it, go forward, like the year that is coming.

Day to day memory, you should cultivate it
So, if possible, it will last a little longer.

We don't know how to appreciate it when we have it,
One day soon we might need it.

To be able to move, to be able to dress
And even to eat, and maybe even to smile.

How difficult is it to live, with nothing to remember!
If yesterday was a happy one or where I am right now...

Memory, like the year, is gone little by little,
Enjoy it always when you can, whatever is left.

LOVE

Even though unexpected events can happen in life, what's important, or at least what's important for me, is that your dreams can come true. For some people that will be to have a family, for others to have a nice house or maybe go on holiday and of course for some it will be all those things and more. In my case, I worked all my life to be able to leave my town. Despite living close to a big city I considered myself a town person; all I had to do was catch the bus and in less than twenty minutes I would be in a major city, but none of it called to me: not its people or its rhythm. There was a university campus nearby that had been set up precisely in this town to avoid having to pay the high prices of the big city. This was reflected in the tuition fees: students didn't have big expenses like in the city. This allowed the university to be a kind of mini-city due to the large area of land it occupied with facuties, laboratories and university residences. So despite being a town. it had all the movement of big city people, especially students from the surrounding areas.

Personally, I would prefer what some call a life in the country air, a farmer's life. But hey, what was I going to do, travel? I have travelled little throughout my life; sometimes because I didn't have enough money and others simply because I didn't know where to go. Although I have seen many documentaries of exoctic places and vacation sites, I didn't imagine myself there doing nothing, losing time over days or weeks. Thinking of being on an island like Fiji or another location like that, well it could be a new experience but there was no attraction in it for me. Spending the whole day lying down by the seashore listening to Hawaiian music or drinking Coco Loco on a Caribbean beach, it could be the most marvellous thing in the world for someone, but for me just walking in nature is enough to relax.

But getting back on topic, what I wanted to share was my desire to travel, or better said the desire to do one journey in life. Of course this wasn't a type of obligation, it was more if I manage it, great, if not, oh well.

I have listened to people who feel a moral or even religious obligation to make a trip to a certain place, as in the case of muslims and the journey to Mecca at least once in their life. It was not the case for me, I only set myself a goal in the touristic sense, but it was economically more difficult to carry out. It was about visiting the greatest monument in history built with love, or at least that's what had been said and remained in people's memory. If we talk about the size of monuments, the pyramids in Central America and Africa would be of the greatest importance. If we talk about age they would also be in first place. But I wasn't an architect or archaeologist, nor was I especially interested in history, merely a curious person that had read and somehow idealised a building. This building is one of the seven wonders of the world, so clearly my opinion about its beauty was not wrong. It's the Taj Mahal in India, a building with no practical use beyond representing an ideal, in this case love. Although knowing the story a little more, one could speak of the loss of said love. The legend is well known and documented, about an Indian prince who married a woman who then died young. The man, driven by longing, desperation or mourning for the loss of his love, ordered the construction of the most majestic palace that he could in honour of his wife. At least that is what is documented in the legend of this place, being one of the most visited palaces in India. I don't know why, but when I found out about this place, I had the idea of seeing it. Of course, India isn't just around the corner and my money didn't let me visit it. This is how it has been for years in which it has remained an idea in my memory like when children answer what they want to be when they grow up and they say a medical vet or a race car driver.

I think the important thing is to have some kind of desire or objective in life and be able to achieve it. For me for a long time photography, or better said portraiture, was my passion; it even became almost like an obsession at times. But this trip was something different. It was a wish

I knew I couldn't fulfil but which stayed with me anyway, waiting for the opportunity to achieve it.

When I found out that the university had organised a trip there, I felt a lot of emotion. Firstly, since it was a group of people travelling at the end of their degree the price was reduced quite a bit. Secondly, someone organising it for me was better: it's not the same going alone. I couldn't imagine being somewhere where I couldn't understand the language or the culture, having to ask someone for help whenever I needed something. I didn't like to ask for help or depend on anyone, so the idea of going in a group where someone else was responsible for solving problems was very reassuring. So, I suppose that final year trip was a glimmer of hope for my dream trip, a trip to the place I was enamoured with the first time I saw a photograph. Or, maybe it wasn't so much the monument that called my attention so much as the history locked inside it.

I still remember the time that a young man came asking for a quickly developed picture for his wife, or rather his future wife. It was a man who seemed to be very excited but nervous about it at the same time. He wanted everything to be perfect for the wedding, or at least that's what he told me though he had participated very little in the actual organisation. Despite the mother of the bride being in charge of most of the ceremony and reception, he still wanted to bring a surprise. Even though he had already bought tickets to spend 10 days on a paradise island, which is what some cultures do to celebrate the honeymoon, he was still looking to do something memorable and beautiful for his wife. He had decided to develop a series of photos from a trip they took to India a few years ago. According to him, he met her on that trip, and this was someone previously too occupied with his books to notice the female gender, so when he finished his course and was free from his books that's when he noticed this girl.

To begin with she didn't pay much attention to him because she had come with a group of girlfriends so she was dedicated to them. But his insistence seems to have paid off since by the end of the trip they had exchanged numbers and had almost started dating. The trip was extremely calm, since they met he hadn't had eyes for another person. He told me that what he liked the most was not only the girl but also the intellect: he could talk to his woman about anything which is not something that happened to him very often. Perhaps it was studying theoretical physics: something that not everyone is interested in and which not everyone fully understands. Plus, despite having finished his exams he was still waiting to find out his results. So he was especially nervous at having gone for a walk, not knowing if he had finished his degree or not. Later he would emigrate to another place for work. This was far from being an advantage for him, it was another source of added stress, since he would now have to go to another place with hardly any money saved despite having benefited from scholarships for his good grades.

But maybe I'll share that story another day. What I wanted to indicate is that, according to what he said to me, there was a group of three girls who approached him to see if he spoke the language and could help them negotiate at the stalls that were on the street. That allowed him to introduce himself and of course he had prepared a few phrases to allow him to communicate with the people in the town. It was nothing more than a curiosity that he had had to be prepared for that trip. Just like he had read about the place he was going to go: the most interesting things and what the dominant culture was, especially in terms of philosophy on life and religion. He had also read some phrases that could be of help to him and it turns out as well as allowing him to negotiate in his own purchases, they also allowed him to meet the person who would one day be his wife. It is not that he had learned a language or any dialect or anything like that, simply the basic words to negotiate, "please, I want that" "how much does it cost?", or "that is very expensive", but since others approached him for the same thing, that first meeting gave more than expected. According to what he told me, it was on one of the bus trips used to move from one city to another, where they had to spend a few hours sitting down, that the connection was established. Where there was a before and after in his life that started as a conversation without much significance.

At first it was just talking for the sake of talking, to fill the time, but as the hours passed, the topics of conversation got more interesting. She was not one of those girls he thought she would be: from a group of cheerleaders characterised by an intense social life and sometimes a not so brilliant school performance. On the contrary, it seemed that she was an extremely remarkable person and yes, clearly he liked her a lot to hang out with her friends. Another thing that he told me about that trip was that they had forgotten the camera at the hotel so they did a kind of money collection from several students to be able to buy a camera to take the photographs with. The reel of group photos the man had brought to be developed were not so strange. The intention was to develop the photos just of the two of them, but particularly those including the Taj Mahal. Visiting that monument was when he realised that their budding friendship could be more, that this woman could be the love of his life, so he wanted to bring some photos of that moment to the wedding which would legalise their relationship. In fact, that culture had such a big impact on them that they had decided to have a hindu style wedding to recreate the feeling of that place, but since he wasn't someone that had a lot of money he had decided to make this photograph as big as possible and give it as a gift.

That's how I found out about the legend of this place and was able to marvel at it. So much so that visiting it became a personal wish that I was finally able to fulfil through university. I don't know what I expected from that place, if I would find love like this couple, but at least I would be able to find out.

Bear in mind that working on photography has allowed me to understand that time comes to everyone, whether they like it or not, and when they die the only thing left behind is the memories of those who knew them, and of course the photographs. The hardship is that at times memories get lost, no matter how long the image in a photo lasts, although sometimes not even these last. So I have been able to see how packets of photos are left on shelves waiting for their owners to collect them. When that didn't happen they were placed in a drawer, after a year there they were destroyed. Nowadays this type of shop has closed down, giving way to digital photos and automated machines, but personally I would prefer my photos to be revealed on paper. This might seem old fashioned or classic, I don't know, but I liked to be able to touch the photo. For sure digital photography allows images to be kept longer and in better quality, but I began in the world of printed photos and I liked to touch them.

But getting back on topic, I have talked with lots of people about what they hope people will remember when they are gone; there are few who really think about it, believing it won't happen to them or maybe it will happen peacefully at night. But they all admit that at least they want their loved ones to have a photo so that they don't forget them. The reality later is that their loved ones don't think or feel the same and simply continue their lives as though nothing has happened.

So many photographs lost! So many stories untold! Stories of people who walked through this world, each one with their own hopes, wishes and desires, some who achieved them and some who stayed on the path. Maybe over time I would start to understand the perspective of those who don't want to be photographed.

Anyway, if any of us were asked about a perfect moment, if such a thing existed, maybe you would choose one from your childhood where there were no worries and you knew that you had the love and support from your parents, or maybe the perfect moment would be the day you met your partner and fate joined you for the rest of your lives. At least that's what you might think, but when I ask people about it, they tell me very different things. It is not that they had a childhood without parental affection or that they aren't in love with their partners, it is just that their perfect moments are about the people who are no longer with them. It is as if the most important thing for them was to go back to the past and have, for a second, a minute, an hour, a day, one more life together with the loved one who has already passed away. Sometimes that was parents, sometimes partners or a child that had passed away, but the person values time with them more than time with people they have left, more than the life they have in the present.

CHAPTER 5. MY OWN PHOTOGRAPHY

Sat by the window, looking out at the sun,
A sudden gust of wind blows through.

A memory of the past comes to mind
When I had little ones and went to the park.

While they played I liked to watch
the shadows moving on the ground.

The wind moved the leaves and when they started to
dance
The sun shining on them projected a thousand pictures.

It was very entertaining, it made me dream
About far away places, or mountains or the sea.

It was the leaf dance, but you could see
Figures dancing to the right and back again.

The same in my window, sat down I remember
Those sunshine dances and my little ones playing.

Where will they be now? Where has the time gone,
Those happy days, the memory remains.

Where will the others be? So many pasts
Those days, those years that oblivion has erased.

What's the point in living if everything is to be forgotten?
It doesn't matter if I was happy, no one is going to
remember.
On the bank of that park, another person will be
Looking maybe at those leaves, at how they dance to the
beat.

From this breeze that plays, and doesn't leave them in
peace
It drags them, takes them away, never to return.

It's just like life, that one day took us
Happily to the park, but that day is over.

Now there are no children, no games and nothing is like
yesterday
Only a distant memory I don't want to lose.

The wind and the sun return, to that park perhaps
but those who were there will never be seen again.

Those children grow up, life takes hold,
Now they don't even see each other; a long time has gone
by.

And maybe in their memory not even the park remains
Not even the games remain, it's in the past.

Here at the window, I have remembered again
seeing the sun and that ray, passing through the glass.

LOVE

Time goes by fast and youth left years ago without me realising. Though I didn't want them to, the years advanced relentlessly and I accumulated many experiences: starting a family, having some children. Adulthood took them far away. Thinking about the future I want to leave a memory. My life wasn't especially remarkable nor was it anything special like the ones that appear on the news and get called anonymous heroes, but I wanted to leave something from my many lived years but I couldn't think how to do it.

It is often said that in life you have to do three things before you die, or at least try to, you have to plant a tree, write a book and have kids. Of the three I had had children, so I still needed to plant a tree or write a book but I wanted to do something different or original and I couldn't think of a better way to do it than through photography. For so many years it had marked my relationship with time, which I had somehow managed to deceive, so that so many who had passed on wouldn't be forgotten through that photo development company.   On more than one occasion I tried to do an exposition or something like it, to record these people that no one knew the names of or where they had lived or what they had done in life. But when I tried I found that the public did not respond as expected, looking at photos of unknown, non-famous people didn't seem to attract them much. From what I understood, that would not be what I was going to leave for the future if someone became interested in what I had done in my own life. After much thought, and despite the doubts that initially sparked in me, I took a photograph.

It's not like I hadn't previously taken many others, but as a photography lover it was something almost mandatory on my part. What was different about this photo was the meaning, if you could call it that, that I wanted to give this photo, where I tried to collect feelings, thoughts and even my story, a photograph that the viewer didn't need explaining. I spent weeks thinking about how to do it and I gathered all the titles and trophies that I had achieved in life and put them together in a glass case. Then I took a photo in front of them as a reminder of my achievements in life and so that anyone who saw the photograph would know that I studied at university, that I got first place in a national championship, and that I was considered the employee of the month on several occasions, quite an achievement on a personal and professional level. But when I looked closely, that photograph seemed quite banal. Who would care that in a company that no longer exists an employee had earned employee of the month?

That's why I wanted to make a different one, and after much thought, I called my children and they came with their grandchildren and I took a picture with all of them together. This was already something memorable, the whole family that I had managed to form and their children, but after looking at it well, it did not say anything special, the photograph reflected the same thing that could be found of any person who had been born, lived and had children in this world.

After taking many photos, none of which convinced me, I came to one that I believed was photography, the one that distinguished me and above all spoke of me.

In one of the rooms of the house I had a room full of photographs of those people forgotten by others but who had contributed important aspects to my life. So, standing in front of hundreds of portraits, I took that photograph. I looked at it and I liked it. That was precisely what I wanted to show: that life is an instant and you should take advantage of it, no matter what you do or who you are with, what you achieve or the family you leave behind. The important thing, for me, is to live it, enjoy it and make others happy, whether they are family members or not. That's what I had managed to show; in that photograph were the portraits of hundreds of people who were no longer there but who were once important to those who knew them.